Ladybird Readers

Heidi

Series Editor: Sorrel Pitts
Text adapted by Sorrel Pitts
Illustrated by Tamsin Hinrichsen
Song lyrics by Pippa Mayfield

LADYBIRD BOOKS

UK | USA | Canada | Ireland | Australia
India | New Zealand | South Africa

Ladybird Books is part of the Penguin Random House group of companies
whose addresses can be found at global.penguinrandomhouse.com.
www.penguin.co.uk   www.puffin.co.uk   www.ladybird.co.uk

Penguin
Random House
UK

First published 2017
Updated version reprinted 2023
005

Printed in China

The authorized representative in the EEA is Penguin Random House Ireland,
Morrison Chambers, 32 Nassau Street, Dublin D02 YH68

A CIP catalogue record for this book is available from the British Library

ISBN: 978-0-241-28433-9

All correspondence to:
Ladybird Books
Penguin Random House Children's
One Embassy Gardens, 8 Viaduct Gardens, London SW11 7BW

MIX
Paper from
responsible sources
FSC® C018179

Heidi

Picture words

Heidi

Grandfather

Aunt Dete

Clara

Peter

goat

mountains

wheelchair

maid

ghost

Heidi lived with her Aunt Dete in a little town in Switzerland. The town was near some mountains.

One day, Aunt Dete said, "Today, we will go and see your grandfather."

Heidi's grandfather lived in the mountains.

7

While Heidi and Aunt Dete were walking up the mountain, they saw a boy called Peter. Peter looked after the goats on the mountain.

They walked to Grandfather's house. He came out to meet them.

"Heidi, I have to go to Frankfurt," Aunt Dete said. "You must stay here with your grandfather."

Heidi's grandfather looked worried.

"She can't stay here," he said. "I'm much too old. How can I look after a little girl?"

But Aunt Dete went back down the mountain, and Heidi stayed with her grandfather.

"Where will I sleep?" she asked.

Grandfather made her a little bed in the roof of the house. Then, Peter gave Heidi some goats' milk to drink.

Heidi was happy living in the mountains with her grandfather. She liked the trees and flowers, and she liked looking after the goats with Peter.

Heidi liked a little white goat the most. She was called Snowflake.

Sometimes, Heidi went to see Peter's grandmother, who couldn't see.

"There are so many beautiful trees and flowers in the mountains," Heidi told her.

One day, Aunt Dete came back from Frankfurt.

"Heidi," she said, "you must go to school."

"Where must I go?" said Heidi.

"To Frankfurt," said Aunt Dete. "I have friends who live there. You will stay with them."

19

Grandfather was very sad, because he loved Heidi.

"Does Heidi have to go?" he said.

Heidi was sad, too. "I want to stay here with Grandfather and Peter," she said.

"No. You must go to school," said Aunt Dete.

Aunt Dete took Heidi to
a big house in Frankfurt.
She lived there with some
of Aunt Dete's friends.

A little girl called Clara lived
there, too. Clara couldn't walk.
She had to sit in a wheelchair.

Heidi liked Clara, but she wasn't happy in Frankfurt. She wanted to go back to Grandfather and Peter in the mountains.

At night, Heidi dreamed about the mountains and Snowflake, the little white goat.

One day, when Heidi came home from school, Clara said, "Last night, the maid saw a ghost on the stairs. Tonight, Daddy won't go to bed because he hopes to see the ghost, too."

That night, Clara's father
waited for the ghost. His friend,
a doctor, waited with him. Soon,
they heard a noise on the stairs.
It was Heidi – she was walking
while she slept!

"So, this is the ghost!" said Clara's
father. "Heidi, you were sleeping
and walking at the same time!"

The doctor took Heidi back
to her bedroom.

"What were you dreaming
about?" said the doctor.

"I was dreaming about the
mountains," said Heidi. "I am happy
here, but I miss my grandfather
and Peter."

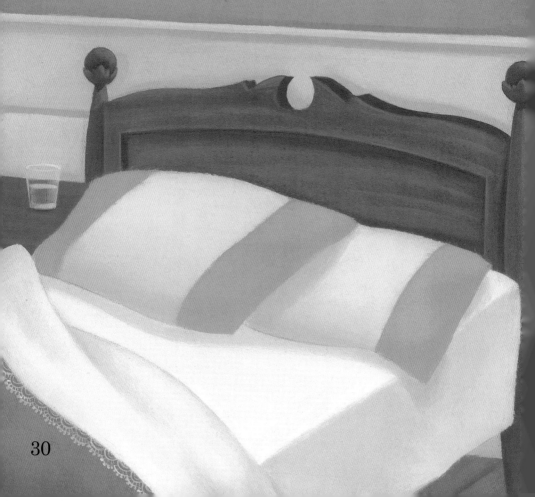

31

Clara's father was worried about Heidi. "I'll take you home," he said.

Heidi went to see Clara.

"I'll miss you," Heidi said. "Please come and see me when I am back in the mountains."

"I'll miss you, too," said Clara. "I'll come and see you soon."

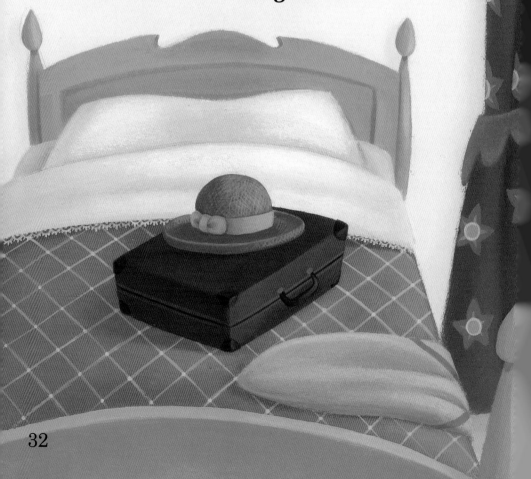

Heidi went back to the mountains. Grandfather and Peter were very happy to see her. Peter gave her some goats' milk. Then, Heidi went to sleep in her little room in the roof.

Heidi didn't walk while she slept that night. She was very happy to be home.

The next day, Heidi looked after the goats with Peter.

"I'm very happy, because you're back," said Peter. "I missed you a lot."

"I missed you, too," said Heidi. "I want to stay in the mountains, and never go back to Frankfurt."

One morning, some people came to the door. It was Clara and her father.

"I have to go to Paris," said Clara's father. "Clara can stay here with you for a week."

Heidi was happy to see Clara. She took her to see all the beautiful things in the mountains.

But Peter wasn't happy to see Clara, because she was always with Heidi. When no one was looking, he pushed Clara's wheelchair down the mountain.

The next day, Clara could not find her wheelchair.

"I must try to walk," said Clara. So, Heidi and her grandfather helped her.

Suddenly, Clara started to walk by herself.

"Look! You can walk!" said Heidi.

Peter was happy, too. "I'm so sorry," he said. "Will you be my friend, Clara?"

The next day, Clara's father came to take her back home. Clara walked out of the house to meet him.

"You can walk!" said Clara's father. "This is the happiest day of my life."

After that, Heidi, Clara, and Peter were always friends.

Activities

The key below describes the skills practiced in each activity.

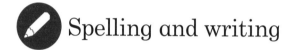 Spelling and writing

Reading

Speaking

Listening*

Critical thinking

Singing*

Preparation for the Cambridge Young Learners exams

*To complete these activities, listen to the audio downloads available at **www.ladybirdeducation.co.uk**

1 **Look and read. Choose the correct words and write them on the lines.** 📖 ✏️ ✿

Clara Grandfather Peter Switzerland

1 The girl in the story who cannot walk.

Clara

2 The country where Heidi lives with Aunt Dete.

3 Heidi's mother's father.

4 The boy in the story who looks after goats.

2 Do the crossword.

Down

1 These animals live on mountains.

2 There was no ghost on the . . .

3 This woman works in a rich person's home.

Across

3 These are very big hills.

4 When you are not with your friends, you . . . them.

5 You feel this when you are not happy.

3 **Look at the letters.**
Write the words. 📖 ✏️

(d i H e i)

1 " <u>Heidi</u>, I have to go to
Frankfurt," Aunt Dete said.

(f a g t r h a e r n d)

2 "You must stay here with your

...."

(e w r i o r d)

3 Heidi's grandfather looked

...."

(y s a t)

4 "She can't .... here," he said.

(h c m u)

5 "I'm .... too old. How can
I look after a little girl?"

49

4 Ask and answer the questions with a friend. 💬 ❓

1

> *Where did Grandfather live?*

> *He lived in the mountains.*

2 Where did Aunt Dete have to go?

3 Where did Heidi sleep?

4 What did Peter give Heidi?

5 **Read the questions.**
Write complete answers.

1 Was Heidi happy living in the mountains?

Yes, she was.

2 Why did Heidi like living there?

3 What did Peter do?

4 Which goat did Heidi like the most?

6 Circle the correct words.

1 Peter's grandmother couldn't

  a see.   **b** walk.

2 Heidi told Peter's grandmother
  about the beautiful trees and
  a flowers.   **b** goats.

3 One day, Aunt Dete came back from
  a Paris.   **b** Frankfurt.

4 Aunt Dete said, "Heidi, you must
  go to
  a my house."   **b** school."

7 **Read the text. Choose the correct words and write them next to 1—5.**

> have to   had to   called   took   stay

"Does Heidi ¹ ___have to___ go?"

said Grandfather. "I want to

² _____ here," said Heidi.

"No, you must go to school," said Aunt

Dete. Aunt Dete ³ _____

Heidi to live in a big house. A little girl

⁴ _____ Clara lived there,

too. Clara couldn't walk. She

⁵ _____ sit in a wheelchair.

8 Talk about the two pictures with a friend. How are they different?

In picture a, the little room is in the roof. In picture b, the room is in Clara's big house.

9 Order the story. Write 1—5. 📖

.... It was Heidi! She was sleeping and walking at the same time.

.... Clara's father and the doctor waited for the ghost.

___1___ The maid saw a ghost on the stairs.

.... Soon, they heard a noise on the stairs.

.... Clara's father took Heidi back to the mountains.

10 Circle the correct words.

1 The doctor took Heidi back to
her bedroom. / **the mountains**.

2 The doctor asked Heidi, "What
were you **screaming** / **dreaming**
about?"

3 Heidi missed her grandfather and
Peter. / **her aunt**.

4 Clara's father was **worried** / **not
worried** about Heidi.

5 Back in the mountains, Heidi
walked / **didn't walk** while
she slept.

11 **Read the story. Write some words to complete the sentences.**

Heidi went to see Clara. "I'll miss you," Heidi said to her friend. "Please come and see me."
"I'll miss you, too," said Clara.
"I'll come and see you soon."
Then, Clara's father took Heidi back to her grandfather.

1 Before Clara's father <u>took Heidi</u> back to the mountains, Heidi talked to Clara.

2 "I'll miss you," _____ Heidi.

3 "I will also _____," Clara told her friend.

12 Listen, and ✓ the boxes. 🎧 ⬤

1 Where did they walk?

ⓐ

ⓑ  ✓

ⓒ

2 Who says this?

ⓐ

ⓑ

ⓒ

3 Who was happy?

ⓐ

ⓑ

ⓒ

4 What did she like?

ⓐ

ⓑ

ⓒ

13 Complete the sentences.
Write a—d. 📖

1 Clara's father had to
go to Paris, so ....c........

2 Heidi and Clara were
happy together, but Peter ....

3 When no one was looking,
Peter pushed ....

4 When Heidi and Grandfather
helped Clara, ...

a was not happy to see Clara.

b she started to walk by herself.

c Clara stayed with Heidi in the
mountains for a week.

d Clara's wheelchair down the
mountain.

14 Listen, and write the answers.

1 Who said this?

Grandfather

2 Who said this?

....

3 Who won't go to bed?

....

4 What was Heidi doing?

....

5 What was she dreaming about?

....

15 **Ask and answer the questions with a friend.** 🗨 ❁

1 *Why didn't Heidi want to stay with Clara's family?*

Heidi missed her grandfather and Peter.

2 Was a week in the mountains with Heidi good for Clara? Why? / Why not?

3 Was it a good thing that Peter pushed the wheelchair down the mountain?

4 How did Heidi change her grandfather's life, do you think?

16 Write about this story.

17 Sing the song.

Heidi went to live with her grandfather.
She liked the trees, she liked the flowers.
She liked her friend Peter, and his goats.
She was happy there in the mountains.
Her aunt said, "Heidi, you must go to school.
You can stay with my friends in Frankfurt."
Heidi liked Clara, her friend in a wheelchair,
but still she dreamed about the mountains.
The maid saw a ghost.
Clara's father wanted to wait for the ghost.
The ghost was Heidi, walking while she slept!
She was dreaming about the mountains!
Heidi went back to her grandfather.
He and Peter were happy to see her.
"I never want to go back to Frankfurt," she said.
"I want to stay here in the mountains."
Clara's father had to go away,
so Clara went to stay with Heidi.
Peter wasn't happy – she was always with Clara!
He pushed Clara's chair down the mountain.
Clara said, "I must try to walk,"
and Heidi and her grandfather helped.
Clara's father saw her walk
and everyone was happy in the mountains!

Level 4

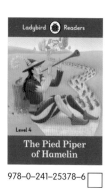

The Pied Piper of Hamelin

978–0–241–25378–6

The Wizard of Oz

978–0–241–25379–3

Sam and the Robots

978–0–241–25380-9

Space

978–0–241–25381–6

Pinocchio

978–0–241–28430–8

Alice in Wonderland

978–0–241–28431–5

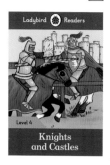

Knights and Castles

978–0–241–28432–2

Heidi

978–0–241–28433–9

Peter and the Wolf

978–0–241–28434–6